The BUS RIDE

written by **WILLIAM MILLER** • illustrated by **JOHN WARD**

introduction by **ROSA PARKS**

LEE & LOW BOOKS Inc.
New York

For my grandmother, Margaret Morgan,
with love and gratitude—W.M.

In memory of my favorite aunt,
Reneé Theresa Glover—J.W.

Lee & Low Books Inc., 95 Madison Avenue, New York, NY 10016
leeandlow.com

Manufactured in China by RR Donnelley Limited, October 2016

Book design by Christy Hale
Book production by The Kids at Our House

The text is set in Goudy
The illustrations are rendered in acrylic paint on canvas

(HC) 10 9 8 7 6 5
(PB) 15 14 13 12 11
First Edition

Library of Congress Cataloging-in-Publication Data
Miller, William.
The bus ride/by William Miller; illustrated by John Ward.—1st ed.
p. cm.
Summary: A black child protests an unjust law in this story loosely based on
Rosa Parks' historic decision not to give up her seat to a white passenger
on a bus in Montgomery, Alabama, in 1955.
ISBN-13: 978-1-880000-60-1 (hardcover)   ISBN-13: 978-1-58430-026-7 (paperback)
1. Afro-Americans—Juvenile fiction. [1. Afro-Americans—Fiction.
2. Race relations—Fiction.] I. Ward, John, ill. II. Title.
PZ7.M63915Gi 1997
[E]—dc21   97-6850   CIP AC

AS A CHILD, one of the earliest lessons I learned from my mother and grandparents was the importance of taking a stand for what is right. I was taught that there comes a time in all of our lives when we have to stand up for what we believe in, even if others are against us.

In the South during the 1950s, African Americans were not allowed to sit at the front of the bus. I rarely rode the bus because I preferred to walk wherever I had to go rather than be treated like a second-class citizen.

In December 1955, while riding the bus in Montgomery, Alabama, I was asked to give up my seat to a white passenger. I refused. I had no idea history was being made. I chose not to move because I was tired of laws that did not treat me like a first-class citizen in my own country.

We have come a long way since then, but we still have far to go. I have great faith that our young people will continue to struggle for freedom as we approach a new century. I encourage all young people to believe in themselves and take a stand for what is right. It is my hope that reading this story will inspire you to learn about the past so you can help make the future better for all people.

God Bless You,

Rosa Parks

Every weekday morning, Sara rode the bus with her mother. They sat in the back, like always, apart from the white people. Sara made faces at the white children who turned around to look at her. The children laughed and made faces too, until their mothers told them to turn around.

"It's always been this way," Sara's mother would say, squeezing her hand. "Just be glad we have a seat to ourselves."

Her mother got off the bus before Sara. She worked in the kitchens of white people while Sara rode alone to her school.

Sara felt sad for her mother. She worked all day and on weekends too, but there was never enough money to buy shoes or a new dress.

One morning, Sara decided to find out what was so much better about the front end of the bus. She stood up and walked down the narrow aisle.

The seats didn't look any different. The windows were just as dirty and the noise of the bus was just as loud. What was all the fuss about?

"Are you lost, little girl?" a white woman asked her.

"No ma'am," Sara said. "I just wanted to see what was so special."

"I think you'd better go back to your seat," the woman said.
By now, everyone was watching Sara. She thought about her mother, how tired she looked at the end of the day. Sara kept on walking, all the way to the front, and sat down across from the driver. She watched him shift gears and turn the big wheel with both hands. He shot her an angry look.

"Little lady," he said. "You sit in the back—you always sit in the back. You know that."

Sara sat still, telling herself that there was no good reason for her to return to her old seat. The bus driver said something to himself and pushed the brake to the floor. The bus stopped suddenly with a long hissing sound.

"If you can't follow the rules," the bus driver said, "then you can walk the rest of the way." He pulled the door open with a bang.

Sara felt lonely and afraid. It would be easy, she thought, to walk down the steps, walk the rest of the way to school. But that was a very long walk. Why should she walk when no other children did?

"You can close the door," Sara said in a small, confident voice. "I'll ride the rest of the way."

The bus driver got up from his seat and stomped down the steps. The white people on the bus were angry. "Hurry up," they shouted. "We're going to be late for work."

The bus driver came back with a policeman.

"What's the problem today?" the policeman asked.

"There's no problem," Sara said, her heart pounding.

"You know what a law is, don't you?"

"Sure I do," Sara replied. "We learn about them in school."

"That's right," the policeman said, smiling. "Well, one of the laws says that your people ride in the back of the bus. So, if you don't want to break a law, you should go back to your seat."

By then a crowd of people had gathered outside. Their voices were loud and angry. Some of them called Sara ugly names, but some told her to keep her seat. "Don't move," a man shouted. "That seat don't care what color your bottom is."

The policeman shook his head sadly and picked Sara up from her seat. He carried her through the crowd to the police station.

Sara started to cry. "Am I going to jail?" she asked. The policeman didn't say anything, but the crowd yelled louder than ever. "Be brave!" a woman yelled. "That jail will do you good," another yelled back.

Inside the police station, Sara sat at a big desk, while the sergeant called her mother at work. A tall man with a camera took Sara's picture. "I'm from the newspaper," he said. "I write stories about people who do brave things."

"This little girl is just confused," the sergeant said, patting Sara on the back with a big rough hand.

The word about Sara spread quickly. Many people came by to look at her. Someone brought her a candy bar. Sara didn't realize how hungry she was until she took a bite. When the candy bar was halfway gone, Sara's mother walked in the door.

"Let's go," she said, reaching for Sara's hand. "I think it's time to let the police go back to chasing real criminals."

"Just make sure your daughter knows where to sit from now on," the sergeant shouted after them.

Outside, the newspaper man took more pictures of Sara and waved goodbye.

"I'm sorry, Mama," Sara said as they pushed through the crowd. "I didn't mean to cause trouble. I just wanted to see what was so special."

"That's all right," her mother said. "You didn't do anything wrong." They walked the rest of the way home without saying a word.

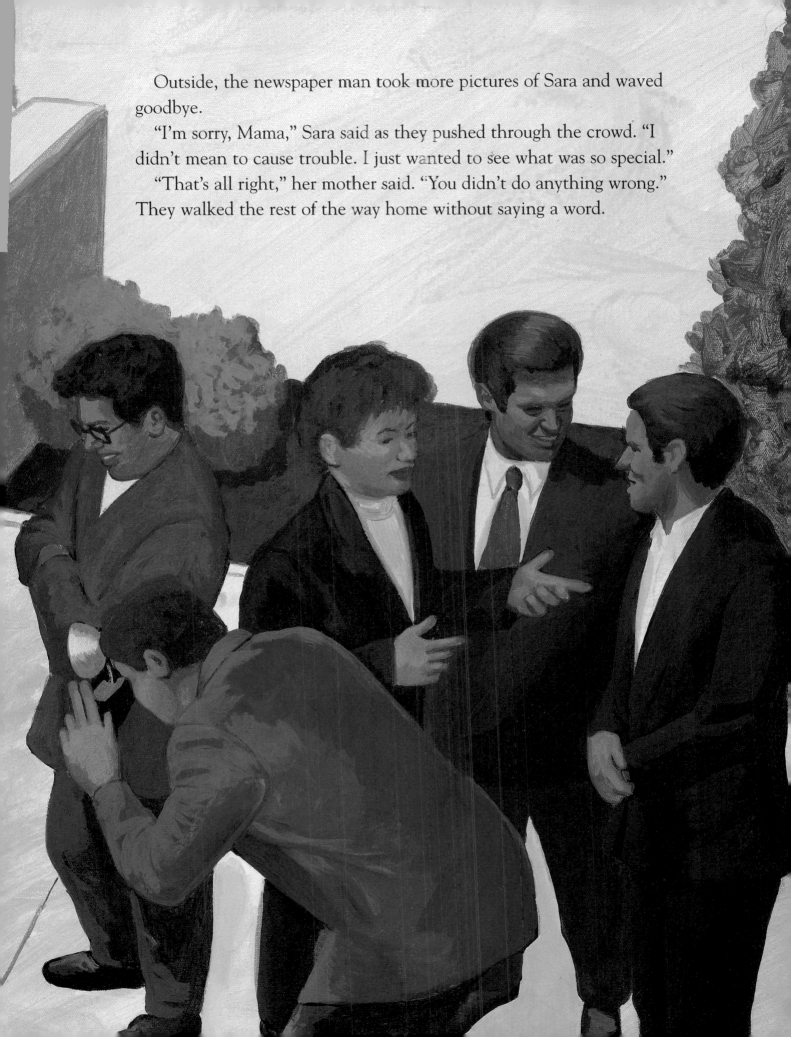

Sara's mother came into her bedroom that night and held her in her arms. "I'm not mad at you, Sara," she said. "You're as good as any white child in this whole, wide world. You're somebody special."

"Then why can't I ride in the front of the bus?" Sara asked, feeling more confused than ever.

"It's the law," her mother said. "But that doesn't mean it's a good law."

"Won't the law ever change?" Sara asked, looking up into her mother's tired eyes.

"Maybe one day," her mother said softly.

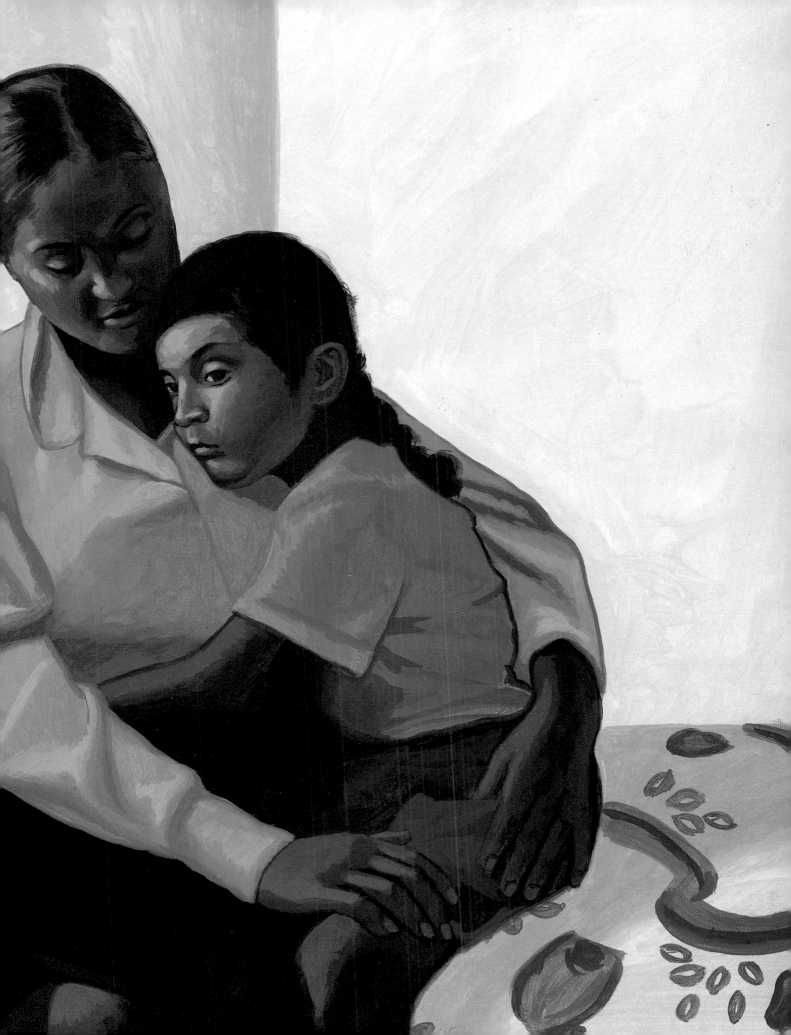

The next morning, Sara's mother asked if she felt like walking instead of taking the bus. Her mother was trying to smile, but Sara saw that there were tears in her eyes.

"It's not such a cold morning anyhow," her mother said. "God gave us two feet—He didn't give us an old bus, now did He?"

"Sure, Mama," Sara said. "I like walking. I don't mind."

Together they strolled past the bus stop. People turned their heads and whispered. A boy Sara's age came running up with a newspaper and a pencil.

"Can I have your autograph?" he asked. Sara's mother took the newspaper from his hand and smiled.

"I guess my little girl's a hero now," she said. Sara looked at her picture on the front page and felt embarrassed.

"Let's go, Mama," she said. But it was too late. Many people, black and white, came up to shake her hand. The newspaper man was back, taking more pictures.

As the crowd walked behind her, Sara began to feel proud. "It's okay to smile," her mother said. "You're somebody special."

No black people rode the bus that day—or the next. The bus company got mad. The mayor got mad. People got so mad they finally changed the law.

"Step right up, little lady," the bus driver said, opening the door. Sara was about to sit down when she turned and looked at her mother. She wore the same coat and the same shoes she had worn for years. But there was something different about her mother today—the pride and happiness in her eyes.

"What are you waiting for, Sara?" she asked. "If anybody ever earned a right to that seat it's my daughter."

The bus driver looked at Sara. The people on the bus looked at Sara.

"No, Mama," she said. "This seat belongs to you!"

Her mother smiled. They sat down together.

The bus rolled forward through the town.